THE DR. CAGE CHRONICLES:
MEMOIRS OF A SEX THERAPIST

First Year Out of the Closet

THE DR. CAGE CHRONICLES:
MEMOIRS OF A SEX THERAPIST

First Year Out of the Closet

GRAYSON ACE

4 Horsemen
Publications, Inc.

This book is dedicated to all of those who support my whore adventures.

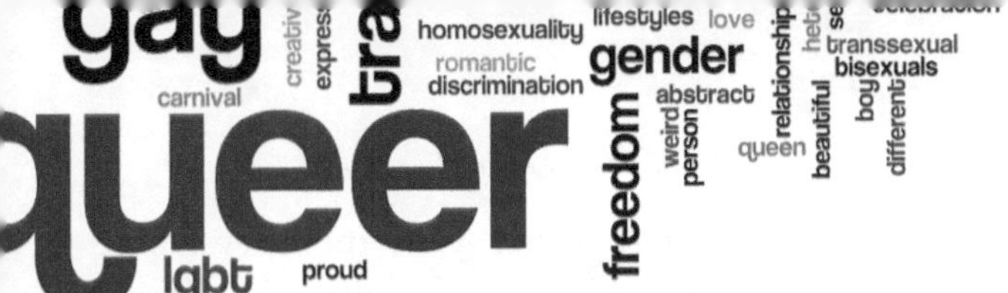

Chapter 1

JACKIE

The minute I arrived in California, I realized that I definitely wasn't in Intercourse anymore. Traffic sucked, a gallon of gas was over $5, and my typical fast food meal ran me $12.95. Luckily, when everything went down with Thomas, I called my best friend Jackie, who was more than happy to let me move in with her and split the rent, which really saved both of us.

Jackie and I have a pretty cool story about how our friendship evolved to where it is today. We've actually known each other since we were little kids. We went to different schools, but we played soccer together. One memory Jackie would tell you about me is that she always knew I was gay because I spent more time on the soccer field bitching about how disgusting it was than actually playing soccer.

We ended up going to high school together, and Jackie became best friends with Elissa, my then-girlfriend. So, through high school and college, Elissa, Jackie, my best friend Mark, and I would all hang out together. We always tried to hook Jackie and Mark up, but it never went anywhere. After Elissa and I broke up and I started dating Thomas, I ran into Jackie at an event in downtown Intercourse. She was running a bar, so Thomas and I went, and it became our normal hangout. Jackie and I started to reconnect, and eventually, we became really good friends.

Of course, right after this happened, Jackie decided she was moving to California, and told me I should move there with her. At the time, leaving Intercourse was out of the question for me because I had just gotten promoted in the practice I was at. Lo and behold, a lot happened over the next nine months, and Jackie finally got her wish.

The gay scene in California was definitely a bit of a shock. The men were beautiful. Because Intercourse was such a small town, and I had only come out to my family a few months before leaving, I never downloaded any of the gay dating apps, or sex apps as I should actually call them. Once I got to California, it was the first thing that I did, and fuck if I didn't feel like the most popular guy in all of California.

That app would go off like crazy all day and all night long. Granted, my little modeling pictures that I had taken right before I left Intercourse definitely helped, and so did the editing. There were so many gorgeous men hitting me up–some were looking for genuine conversations, and some were just on there looking for hook-ups. I'll be honest: I wasn't sure what I was on there looking for. I definitely considered myself to be a relationship man, but I was also looking at this as my opportunity to be a whore in a new city where no one would judge me. Well, at least no one who knew me like everyone back home.

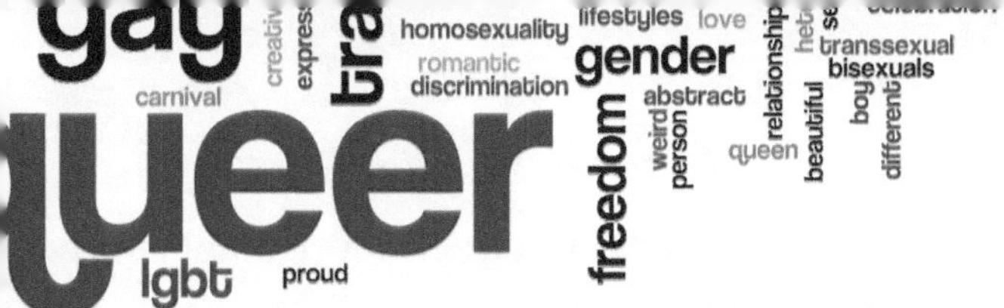

Chapter 2

MICHAEL

Let me tell you about Michael. He was the first guy I hooked up with after moving to California, and to this day, I'm still surprised that I picked him to be my first. Michael was a year younger than I was, and I never even considered talking to someone younger back home because of my maturity level. He wasn't educated and worked part time at a grocery store. He had this beautiful head of hair that he would flip over to one side and a pierced nose. I hated facial piercings. But Michael was extremely cute, and he had a nice body and lips

3

I knew I wanted to taste from the moment I saw him on the app.

The first time we met in person was at a storage facility. Michael actually agreed to help me unload my moving truck into the unit. It was a bit awkward. He showed up, we hugged, and then we immediately got to unloading the truck, not really talking that much because it was so hot. We unloaded for about an hour, and then stood by the truck and made small talk. Jackie and I had moved into a high rise with a roof-top pool, so I asked Michael if he wanted to come over that night to hang by the pool.

Later that night, Michael came over, and we grabbed a few beers and headed up to the pool. Michael took off his shirt, and the first thing I noticed was this amazing chest tattoo that wrapped up his shoulder and down his arm. He had a six pack, and I used the tattoo as an excuse to get closer and touch his chest. It was pretty late, so we were the only ones at the pool. I took my shirt off and dove in, and Michael shortly followed.

We hung in the pool for about a half hour, kind of flirting with each other, splashing around a little bit and occasionally touching. I told Michael that he had beautiful lips and I wanted to kiss them, and Michael responded by asking what took me so long. I swam over in front of Michael, backed him into the corner of the pool and pulled his face close to mine. I said I was waiting for him to make the move, and then we started making out.

My initial thoughts were right. He had the most amazing lips, perfect for kissing. I thought they would be pretty good at some other things too. He shoved his tongue deep in my mouth and rubbed his hands on the back of my head and my back while we kissed. I got a little nervous thinking someone might come out, but I also really didn't care. My cock was quickly getting hard. I grabbed him by his hips and pulled him closer to me. I wanted to feel his cock rubbing against mine. Just as I had thought, he was rock hard. I reached down on the outside of his shorts to feel for his dick. From what I was feeling, he had a pretty nice package, which was impressive for a guy his size. He was muscular, but he wasn't a big guy by any standard. We made out for a few more minutes, and then I finally said we needed to go inside.

We got out of the pool, both of us trying to fix our boners that were showing through our shorts. I started drying off, and Michael came up to me and started kissing me again. I pushed him away and told him to dry off so we could get inside. We grabbed the few beers that were left over and headed inside.

Luckily, Jackie wasn't home because I knew she'd have something to say about me bringing someone home so soon. We went into my bedroom, and I could barely get the door shut before Michael was already taking off his shorts. He jumped on the bed and told me to get naked. I quickly took off my shorts and jumped right onto the bed. I laid down on my back and pulled him over on top of me and started making out, my hands going all over his body. He rolled himself over and pulled me with him, so now I was on top of him. I started kissing his neck, and slowly work my way to his chest. I sucked on his nipples a little bit and started kissing my way down his ripped abdomen to that big thick cock of his. I could feel his cock rubbing on my chin as I got closer, and I let my facial har tickle it a little bit.

I looked up at him and gave him a little grin, and then put his cock as far in my mouth as I could before closing my lips on it. His cock was pretty thick, but I started sucking up and down on it. It tasted so good and was the absolutely perfect size. Michael was pretty loud, and every moan he let out made me think he was going to blow his load. I turned myself around and got on my side so we could get into the 69 position, and Michael's mouth latched onto my cock like a magnet on a fridge. He was a pretty good cock sucker, and we sucked on each other for a few more minutes. I started playing with his ass a little bit while I was sucking on his dick, and right as I had the tip of my finger on his hole, he told me he wanted me inside of him.

I immediately jumped off the bed and grabbed my lube and a condom. I ripped the condom open and started to put it on, but Michael grabbed it off my dick and threw it across the room. He said he wanted to feel my load inside of him, and I was more than willing to give it. I jumped back on the bed with my back up against the pillow. He grabbed the lube and rubbed it on my cock, and then put some on his hole. He kneeled over me and slowly sat his fine ass down on my throbbing cock. He clearly was used to have dicks up his ass because he didn't have that normal hesitation when you first feel the head get inserted. He didn't even give his hole a few seconds to get used to the size of my cock. As soon as it was in, he was riding like he was at the rodeo.

Michael would occasionally lean down and make out with me while I was fucking him, but for the most part, he would grab onto my chest, make really loud moans, and tell me how good my dick felt. I would stroke his dick a little bit, but he would bat my hand away, making me know that every stroke got him closer to cumming. I'm surprised how long I was able to last because his hole was nice and warm and super smooth.

I decided to lean forward a little bit and start sucking his dick while I was fucking him. I grabbed his lower back right above his ass and kind of pulled him a little closer to me as he was riding my dick, and let his cock go in and out of my mouth. I knew I was getting close, and I could feel his cock starting to throb, so I grabbed onto his cock so that I was stroking it and sucking it, his thrusts into my mouth matching mine into his ass. He yelled out that he was going to cum, and his hot load started shooting into the back of my throat. Not even five seconds after he shot his load into my mouth, I started shooting mine into his ass. I still had his cock in my mouth and was trying to swallow his cum, but the orgasm I was having was pretty intense, and my need to let out a loud moan of relief also let about half of his cum drip down my chin and onto my chest.

I kind of held his body up so I could take control of the thrusts because I wanted my cum to go deep inside of him. He was still on top of me, but I started doing the work with my hips so I could really pound my dick hard up his hole. Michael was letting out some pretty loud screams, and a few seconds later, I kind of collapsed on the bed in exhaustion. He leaned forward and kissed me, my dick still inside of him. He then went down towards my chest and started licking up his cum that I had spit out of my mouth. Not going to lie—it was pretty hot to see a guy do that.

Michael ended up spending the night, and we cuddled and made out all through the night.

He had to work early the next morning, and to my surprise, I woke up to him sucking my dick. He told me he wanted one more load before he had to go to work. Not sure how long he had been sucking it for, but I was pretty close, so I just let it go in his mouth. He seemed a bit surprised, swallowed all of it, and then laughed and said he meant he wanted my load in his ass.

"Oops, my bad," I said.

He wiped his mouth off on my pillowcase, gave me a kiss, hopped out of bed, and said "thanks." We both laughed, and that's when I realized young guys weren't too bad after all.

Chapter 3

THE RANDOMS

Obviously as soon as Michael left and went home, I opened up my dating apps to see what was going on. I liked Michael, and maybe it would lead somewhere, but I wanted to find as much dick as I possibly could before settling back down to just one. And after being with Thomas, I told myself I'd never have any type of orgies again *during* a relationship, but while being single? That was another story.

I hooked up with quite a few guys during my first month in San Francisco. I mean, why not? I was single, the men were gorgeous, and we were all horny all of the time. I met this married guy on one of the apps. He wanted to come over on his way home from work. When I opened my door, he was quite different looking than in his photos, but still pretty cute. We went into my bedroom, and he was already hard when he took his pants off, so I didn't even bother sucking his dick. I lubed it up, got on top, and started riding him. Two minutes later, he asked where he could cum, and I told him he could cum inside my ass. He got this really weird grin on his face and came five seconds later. I kept riding him while I stroked my cock, and it only took me another 30 seconds before I shot my load on his face. I got off the bed and threw him his pants. He put on his clothes, we had an awkward conversation, and he left. Fucking him was really nothing to write home about. I thought my first time with a married man would be so much more exciting, but I was pretty disappointed.

Then there was another guy who was in town on business and asked me to come over to his hotel and fuck. I wanted him to come to my place because I knew I'd have to pay for parking if I went to his hotel, but he insisted. I parked my car, and the sign said the first 30 minutes were free, and then anything over that was a flat $30 rate. When I got up to his room, I told him I could only stay for 25 minutes because I had some place to be. What I didn't want to tell him was that I barely had any money because I still hadn't found a job at a new practice and really didn't want to waste money on parking.

Right after I told him I couldn't stay long, he pulled me closer and started making out with me. We kissed for a few minutes, and I told him I wanted to fuck. He laid down on the bed and put on a condom. I grabbed the lube, got on top of him, and started riding his dick. His cock was pretty big – probably about 9 inches, thick, and with a massive left hook. Honestly, though, it didn't feel any different than any other dick I had taken. I rode him for a few minutes, and he started stroking my cock.

I took his hand off my dick and told him if he kept touching it that he was going to make me cum. He grabbed it again anyway and started stroking it. I really didn't care. If he wanted to make me cum, then he could make me cum.

He stroked my cock for another two minutes while I rode him like a cowboy, and I told him I was about to cum. He said he wasn't ready to cum, and I said, "Too bad." He let go of my cock, so I started stroking it myself. Within seconds, I let out a loud scream and started shooting my load all over his chest. I was still kind of bouncing up and down on his dick, and once I was done cumming, I started to get off of him. He grabbed my hips and said he wanted to keep fucking. I told him I really couldn't keep fucking once I had an orgasm because the feeling is too sensitive for me at that point. Once I cum, I'm done (as a bottom anyway).

He seemed disappointed but asked if I would blow him since he couldn't keep fucking me. I really didn't want to. Once I have an orgasm, I kind of lose all interest in any other sexual activity. I didn't want to be greedy though, so I agreed. I told him to go over to the couch. He sat down, and I knelt in between his legs. I pulled the condom off his curved dick, grabbed the base, and started sucking on it. As soon as I put it in my mouth, he started moaning, even though I could barely get that monster in my mouth. I sucked on it for about five minutes, but he didn't seem like he was anywhere close to cumming. I looked at my phone and realized I was about to run out of free parking. I told him I was sorry and that I had to go, but that he should call me next time he was in town. I didn't expect him to call, but I figured it was a nice gesture.

I put on my clothes, gave him a kiss goodbye, and left. As I got on the elevator, my lips started to get a little tingly. I didn't think much of it, but by the time I was walking towards the parking garage, they were almost completely numb. I realized that dick must have used some type of de-sensitizing lotion on his dick, and that's why he couldn't cum. What the fuck? The point of fucking is to cum! I wiped my lips on my shirt but knew I was going to have to just deal with it. I got in my car and put the ticket in the gate. I was over the free parking period by two minutes. $30 wasted, and I didn't even get a good fuck out of it. Maybe the guys in Cali weren't that exciting after all?

Chapter 4

JAKE

I started getting a little stir crazy in San Francisco, and I missed my family really badly. Part of me was questioning my decision to leave my home and move there. I got hired at a small family practice, but I only kept the job for two weeks because their business practices were super unethical. They wanted me to bill each session as a double session, which essentially doubled the practice's profit. I kept playing it off, "Oops, I forgot," but when they threatened to fire me, I told them to go fuck themselves and walked out. I never turned them in, but it didn't even matter because a few weeks later they were audited by the state and were forced to shut down.

I spent my days lying by the pool, drinking beer, and catching up on some good reading. Naturally, I spent several hours a day surfing the apps to see if anyone new and interesting had joined. One morning, I got a message from a guy named Jake. He was pretty cute, and he had a decent body and some very strong Italian features.

His first message was very blunt: "Hey, you're cute. Wanna fuck?"

I had never had someone be so direct and to the point on these apps, but honestly, if a hook-up is all you're looking for, then I can appreciate the bluntness.

I responded and said, "Yeah! Top or bottom?"

He said he was a top, and he lived just a few blocks away from me, which was super convenient. He asked if I could come over in an hour, so I got out of the pool, dried off, showered, and headed toward his place.

Jake lived in a pretty nice complex on the third floor. I knocked on his door, and he answered in just gym shorts. He had a bit of a belly but really nice arms and an overall good body. He was the type of guy that I was attracted to—the "dad-bod" type. I had never asked his age, but from his looks, he was about the same age as I was, maybe a few years older. I walked in, and he just started making small talk.

He led me into his living room, and I noticed there was a sheet down on the floor in front of his couch. On the sheet were a few sex toys and a big bottle of lube. Most guys mention on the apps if they're into sex toys, but I was kind of intrigued by what his thoughts were. He noticed me looking at the toys, and then said he hoped I didn't mind that he wanted to use them. I just shrugged my shoulders. It wasn't like I had never used any kind of toys before.

As I started taking off my shirt, Jake knelt down on the sheet, grabbed my hips, and pulled me closer to him. He looked up at me and started rubbing on my cock through my pants. I pulled my shirt off, threw it on the couch, grabbed the back of his head, and rubbed it while he started unzipping my pants. He pulled my pants down and tugged my cock through the opening of my briefs and started sucking on it. This guy was an awesome cocksucker. His mouth was so warm and wet, it almost felt like fucking an ass.

He was going up and down my shaft pretty slowly, and I could feel the head of my cock going into his throat, which wasn't making him gag at all. He'd pull my cock out of his mouth and start sucking on my balls, stroking my cock, and looking straight up at me. He was making a lot of noises while he was doing this, and I could tell that he was a little bit of a pig.

I pushed him away from my cock and kind of forced him down on the ground. He was wearing a jockstrap, and I pulled his cock out from it and started sucking on it. His dick was pretty average, so I'm glad he wasn't looking to fuck me. I sucked on his cock for a while and then lifted his legs above my head to arch his ass up a bit so I could start licking his hole. He had just a tiny bit of hair on his hole, which was a total turn on for me. I stuck my tongue in as deep as I could get it, and he started panting like a dog. The noises were a bit distracting but also a turn on at the same time.

I licked his hole for a few minutes, occasionally sticking the tip on my finger inside, and then Jake grabbed a dildo and handed it to me. He said he wanted me to fuck him with the dildo while he sucked my dick. He was still lying on the ground, kind of arched up on the couch, and I got on my knees and moved toward his face. Before I could stick the dildo in his ass, he grabbed the bottle of lube and literally poured it all over his chest. He then poured it over mine and started rubbing it all over my chest and cock with his hands. For a second, I thought he was going to want to wrestle.

I ran my hand across his chest to get some of the lube and rubbed it all over his dildo. I leaned over and slowly pushed it into his ass. He let out a loud moan and then grabbed my dick and started sucking on it. I moved the dildo in and out of his ass in a pretty normal pace, and he grabbed onto my hand and made me start thrusting it faster and faster. He kept on sucking my dick the entire time, and I was basically beating his hole with the dildo. He grabbed the dildo from me and pulled it out of his ass and threw it across the room, looked at me, and said, "Fuck me now!" He was still panting and a bit out of breath.

He turned over and got on all fours, so I would fuck him from behind. He leaned over the seat of the couch, and I got up behind him and slid my dick right into his hole. I didn't even need to add any extra lube because we had it all over our bodies. Plus, my dick was dripping from him sucking on it. I grabbed onto his hips and thrust my cock in and out of his hole, just letting the head almost completely come out before shoving it back inside. I could tell he really liked this. I fucked him like this for a few minutes, and then he turned around and asked if I wanted to try a double-ended dildo.

I had never used a double before, but it sounded like it could be a pretty good time, especially with a pig like this. I laid down on the sheet with my head against the couch and let him take control because I knew he was a pro at this. I spread my legs, and he got in front of me with his legs wrapped over mine and our dicks and balls basically touching. This double dildo was about 18 inches long, and not too thick, but thick enough to feel good. He poured more lube on us and then wiped it all over the dildo. He slid it in my ass first, and my cock instantly shot up to attention. He then put the other end in his ass and almost instantly started moving his hips back and forth, which made the dildo start moving a little bit inside my ass.

The dildo felt incredible once I started moving my hips with his. I grabbed onto my cock and started stroking it while I was being dildo fucked. It felt like I was really taking it up the ass. He was still letting out loud moans, and between the dildo, our hips moving, and our legs rubbing against each other, I was completely turned on. We stayed like this for five or six minutes, and any time I let go of my cock, he would grab onto it and stroke it. I'm not sure how I wasn't already cumming, but I must have mentally known he was going to want me to fuck him again.

Jake stopped moving his hips and slowly pulled the dildo out of my ass. I didn't even say anything–I just stayed on my back waiting to see what his next move was. He pulled the dildo out of his own ass and came over and started sucking my dick again. This dude must have really liked the taste of lube because he was slobbering all over my cock. He brought his head up and said, "Fuck me again."

I quickly got up and got behind him. He was on all fours again, so I just shoved my cock right in his ass and started pounding the fuck out of him. I could tell I was getting close to cumming, so I pulled out, grabbed the dildo, and started fucking him with his dildo. He kept on moaning and really liked it, probably because the dildo was just about the same size as my cock. I pushed it in and out for about a minute so I could re-gain some composure in my own dick. I was having way too much fun to cum and didn't want to stop.

I flipped him over on his back and put his legs above my shoulders. He grabbed my cock and guided it into his hole. At this point, his hole was pretty stretched out from my cock and the different dildos, so I knew I probably could fuck a while longer without risking shooting my load. He pulled me down and started kissing me while I was fucking him and kept making a lot of moaning and grunting noises.

After about another seven minutes of him grunting and me going to pound town on his ass, I knew I was getting close to cumming. He started stroking his cock and came about ten seconds later. About half of his cum shot up on my chest, which was really hot. I told him I was about to cum, and he told me he needed me to pull out. I was actually somewhat surprised. I thought for sure a little pig like this was going to want my load inside of him. It wasn't a big deal though because I liked seeing my cum shot anyway.

I kept fucking him, and just as I was about to cum, I pulled my cock out of his ass. I didn't even have to grab my cock to jerk it to the finish–I immediately started shooting my load all over. I mean, my cock barely came out of his ass when it started exploding, and I probably even came inside of his hole a little bit. I backed away from him a little bit and watched as my load shot up and over his head all over the cushions of his couch. He grabbed my cock and started stroking it, and I must have shot eight or nine good loads before it finally died down.

He pulled me down and held me close to him with our bodies, lube and cum rubbing together. It was now a bit awkward, so I got up and said I was going to shower. When I came out of the shower, he had a new sheet on the floor, and the bottle of lube and toys were all lined up in a neat row. This bitch was about to have another dude over, and I was pretty impressed.

Chapter 5

JUAN

 B ack in Intercourse, I really never went to the gay bars. Well, gay bar. There was only one, and it was pretty seedy. Thomas and I had gone a few times, although it was like pulling teeth to get him to go. After we broke up, I realized he was afraid to go to the gay bar because we'd run into all the guys he was fucking around with while we were together, and one of them was bound to say something to me. The main reason I never went was because I only came out to my family a few months before I moved to California, and I was always afraid of running into someone that knew my parents.

San Francisco was full of gay bars, and I went pretty frequently when I first moved there. I would bounce around from bar to bar to just get a feel for the vibes and see which one I liked the most. After being in San Fran for a couple weeks, there was one bar that I found myself coming back to pretty often. The music was good, the boys were pretty, and the bartenders were very friendly. There was one bartender in particular, Juan, who would always strike up a conversation whenever I was there. He was tall, extremely muscular, and had a huge tattoo going down his right arm.

Michael and I would sometimes go to the bar together, and I always had a really good time with him. One Saturday night, I asked him if he wanted to go with me, but his sister was in town visiting him from Chicago, and he couldn't hang out. I was in the mood for some drinks, so I went by myself.

I was pretty comfortable being at a bar by myself. I knew if I sat at the bar and ordered a drink that someone was bound to start talking to me. As soon as Juan saw me sitting at the bar, he grabbed my beer and brought it over to me. He asked me where my boyfriend was, referring to Michael, and I quickly corrected him and told him that we were just friends. Sure, we hung out quite a bit, but we never put a label on us, and we didn't establish any rules. Juan looked at me and smiled, and then had to go help some other customers.

I had quite a few beers that night, and Juan was being super flirty with me. I asked him why he waited until now to start flirting with me. He said he wanted to be respectful because he thought Michael and I were together, and that I was the most attractive guy he had ever seen in his bar. That was a pretty bold statement and made me feel pretty good about myself. He then leaned over the bar and whispered in my ear, "Come back to my place tonight." I had no objections at all, and said, "OK."

The bar started dying down pretty early, and Juan came over to me and said he was able to leave early. I chugged the rest of my beer and went to hand Juan my credit card, but he wouldn't take it. Apparently, hitting on the bartender was going to pay off. We walked out into the parking lot, and Juan told me to follow him. I really shouldn't have been driving, but I also didn't care because I knew where this was going.

We got to Juan's place, and the minute I walked inside, he started to kiss me. He was a good six inches taller than I was, so he had to bend down to make it happen. As we were making out, we slowly made our way into his bedroom and onto the bed. Juan sat down on the edge of the bed, and I stood in front of him and kept shoving my tongue down his throat. He was an excellent kisser, and the buzz I had going made it feel somewhat euphoric. I started crawling onto him and pushed him back on the bed. He quickly grabbed me and flipped me over onto my back and got on top of me and started sucking on my neck. I could feel my nails ripping into his back because it felt so good.

I started moving my hands down to his waist and around the front of him so I could grab his cock. I was still fully clothed, and he was in the gym shorts he had worn to work. I could tell he was hard from when his cock was rubbing on my leg, and when I grabbed onto it through his shorts, I literally stopped kissing him and said, "Oh fuck." He laughed and little bit and asked if everything was alright. I quickly said yes and pulled his head back toward mine so we could keep kissing. The reason I said what I said was because I knew his cock was going inside of me, and I was afraid it was going to hurt–I could tell, even through his shorts, that he had the biggest cock I'd ever seen.

Juan was still on top of me making out, and I started pushing his shorts and briefs down with my hands. I had to see exactly what he was working with. Just as I got his briefs off of him, I pushed him over onto his back and took my shirt off. There it was–a cock the size of a $5 footlong. I grabbed onto the base of it and put his head in my mouth and started sucking on it. I could barely fit any of it in my mouth, but it must have felt good to him because he was moaning. I sucked on it for just a couple minutes because I was eager to get it in my ass.

I told him I was going to have to ride him because I was afraid it was going to hurt, and he just smiled and said that he would be gentle. He got out of the bed and went into the bathroom, returning with a condom and some lube. I sat on the bed just staring at his enormous cock as he put on the condom and lubed it up. He walked toward me and stuck his fingers down below my balls to lube up my ass, and even his fingers felt amazing.

Juan got on the bed and propped up the pillows behind him so he could be sitting somewhat upright. I threw my leg over him and grabbed onto his cock and lined it up with my hole. I slowly sat down on it, and for the first time since I lost my ass virginity, this actually hurt. I put the head in and let my hole get used to his size for a minute, before lowering my ass completely down. I was impressed that Juan didn't try to take control and immediately start thrusting. I'm assuming he was used to his size and guys not being able to take it like champs.

Once I got his entire cock inside of me, I leaned toward him and started making out with him. I needed a minute to let my hole stretch out a bit. I told Juan I was good, and he started pumping his cock in and out at a pretty slow pace. It felt really good, and almost felt like we were making love. Juan was a very passionate person, and he even fucked like one. After a few minutes, I started to take control and started really riding his cock. I was impressed with myself that it stopped hurting so quickly, and it actually felt amazing. After a few minutes of riding him, I asked if he wanted to take the condom off. He said he only put the condom on because he assumed I wanted him to. I told him I'd much rather feel his bare cock inside of me.

I got off his dick, and I could tell my hole was pretty gaping. I pulled the condom off his dick and threw it across the room. Juan got up from his position and stood next to the bed and pulled me over to the edge. He pushed me down on my back and lifted my legs above his shoulders. He put some more lube on his cock before putting it back inside of me. He was fucking me faster than he was when I was riding him, and it felt so good. I started stroking on my cock, and I knew I wasn't going to last very long. Another two minutes of his massive cock inside of me, and I was ready to blow. I told him I was about to cum, and just as I started shooting my load on my chest, he pulled his dick out of my ass and shot his load on my cock and chest. He was a pretty decent shooter and some of his cum even came up and landed on my face, which I happily pushed into my mouth so I could taste it.

Juan walked over to the bathroom and grabbed a towel and brought it back to me so I could clean up. He asked me if I wanted to stay the night with him, and I smiled because I was hoping he would ask that. We got in the shower together and cleaned each other's bodies, making out almost the entire time. We got into bed, and he quickly put his arm around me and pulled my head onto his chest. His muscular body felt so good wrapped around mine and made me feel so safe.

I slept like a baby that night, but when I woke up in the morning, I was in bed by myself. I got out of bed and noticed a note on the nightstand that said, "Went for a run. Make yourself at home." I wanted to stay, but I really needed to get home. I grabbed my phone and my keys, and as I walked out the door and looked at my phone, I saw I had 15 missed calls—from Michael.

Chapter 6

CHRIS

I texted Michael back and made up some lie that my phone was acting up. I didn't owe him anything, but I also didn't want to tell him the truth and make him mad or jealous. I know I'd probably be jealous if I knew he was out fucking someone else.

Jackie and I were living in a high-rise right downtown. I could see the apartments from where I parked in the parking garage, and then I had to walk across a bridge to get into the building. Whenever I would park my car, I would notice this guy out on his balcony two floors above mine. He'd wave, and I would wave back, and that was about it.

One night when I was browsing through the apps, a message popped up from a guy named Chris. It said he was 25 feet away from me, so I assumed it had to be the guy who was always on his balcony waving at me. Chris was about three years younger than I was, but he had the body of a Greek God. He was absolutely ripped and had huge arms and was just an adorable guy.

Chris and I would chat just about every day, and after a couple of days, he told me he was living with his boyfriend. I asked him why he was on these apps if he had a boyfriend, and he said that he was just looking for more friends. I was a little bummed because he was super cute, and potentially good boyfriend material, but I guess none of that mattered. He invited me over for drinks one night, and I happily accepted.

When I got to Chris's apartment, his boyfriend answered the door. His boyfriend definitely wasn't the kind of guy I'd expect Chris to go for. He was super feminine acting, very skinny, and honestly just seemed like a bitch. We had a few drinks and talked for a little bit, but I really didn't want to be around his boyfriend, so I made up an excuse about having to be up early the next day and left.

The next night Christ messaged me and asked if he could come over to my place for a drink. I asked if he was bringing his boyfriend, but he said that he was working. I really didn't want to hang out with his boyfriend. Chris came over with a six-pack in his hand, and we just sat in the living room and talked. After about ten minutes, Chris asked if he could see my bedroom. I didn't really think much of it, and I got off the couch and led him toward my room. I walked in first, and when he followed me in, he shut the door behind me.

I asked him what he was doing, and he responded, "What I've wanted to do since I saw you." He sat his beer down on the dresser, pushed me against the bed, and started kissing me. I pushed him away and asked about his boyfriend, but he said he didn't care. Honestly, neither did I, so I grabbed him by the back of his head and pulled him in. We started making out. It was one of those super-fast, super intimate makeout sessions where we were ripping our clothes off as fast as we could while still kissing.

I was still leaning against the bed, and when Chris pulled his underwear off, I saw that he was already hard, and he had a beautiful thick cock that must have been about eight inches. I quickly got down on my knees and started sucking his dick. He leaned forward a bit and put his hands on the bed to sort of hold himself up. He was moaning pretty loud, and I could feel his dick pulsing in my mouth. I kept sucking on it, and after about two minutes, he shot his load down my throat. I was actually kind of glad that he came so quickly because I really wasn't in the mood to fuck.

I swallowed his load, and when I stood up, he looked at me and said, "We shouldn't have done this." I could tell he felt guilty, and he quickly put on his clothes and left. I kind of felt a little bit used but also didn't really care because he was so hot.

The next day Chris messaged me and asked if we could talk. I asked if he wanted to come over to my place, but he said he wanted me to come over to his. That night, I went over to his place, and I assumed his boyfriend was at work. It made sense because I didn't think he'd ask me to come over to talk if his boyfriend were home. I walked in, and Chris handed me a beer. He made small chit-chat, and I was waiting for him to bring up what happened the night before, but he never did.

After about a half hour of talking about pretty much nothing, Chris said that he was feeling really tense in his shoulders and back and needed to book a massage. I responded by telling him that I was a pretty good masseuse, and Chris said, "Oh, prove it." He got up and motioned for me to follow him, and we went into his bedroom. To my surprise, there was a candle lit on the nightstand and a bottle of massage oil next to it.

Had he been planning this? I thought he felt bad about what happened the night before.

Chris took his shirt and shorts off, only leaving his briefs on, and laid down on his stomach. I really didn't notice his muscular back or his fine ass the night before, but damn. I grabbed the oil off the nightstand, and as I went to get on the bed to started, he said, "Wait. Can you take your clothes off too? It relaxes me." I didn't even hesitate, and quickly took off my shirt and shorts, only leaving on my briefs. I came up behind him, somewhat straddling his ass and poured some oil on his back.

As I was massaging his back, he was letting out some soft moans. I rubbed his shoulders for a while, and then worked my way down to his lower back. Every time I got down to his lower back, I would put my hands inside of his briefs a little bit to be able to feel his ass. At this point, my dick was hard, and I knew his had to be to. I got up for a second and pulled his briefs off, and I took mine off too before getting back on top of him. When I got back on him and my hard cock hit his ass, he arched his back a little bit as to raise his ass into my cock.

I moved down a bit, so I could start massaging his ass. s I was rubbing it, I could see how perfect of a hole he had, and I knew I needed to taste it. I moved down a little bit more, spread his cheeks, and started to slowly move my tongue from the base of his balls up to his hole. Chris let out a loud moan and pushed his head farther into his pillow. I put my tongue as deep into his ass as I could, and he tasted so clean and so good. He arched his back and pushed his ass into my face, and I could tell he wanted me deeper. As he raised his hips, I grabbed onto his rock-hard cock and started stroking it while I kept licking his hole. After a few minutes, I knew I wanted him inside of me.

I let go of his cock and grabbed his hips to turn him over on his back. I poured the massage oil on his cock and rubbed some on my hole to get it ready. I leaned forward and started kissing him as I straddled his cock and lowered my ass onto it. His cock slid in with such ease–maybe I was still loose from Juan. As soon as his cock was all the way inside of me, his eyes got really big, almost like they were going to come out of his head. He said that his boyfriend never rode his dick and would only let him fuck him on his back.

I knew Chris wasn't going to last very long, and neither was I, so I grabbed his hand and put it on my cock so he could stroke it while I was riding his. He felt so good, and I knew I could ride his perfect cock for hours, but I also knew that wasn't going to happen. After about three minutes of taking that dick up and down, he said he asked where he should cum. I told him I wanted him to shoot his load up my ass. When I said that, he let go of my cock and grabbed my hips and took control. He started fucking me faster, and I started stroking my own dick. Within seconds, he let out the loudest moan I think I had ever heard, and I knew he was filling me up. I could tell I was about to cum, and when I'm bottoming, I really never ask, because I feel like I don't have to. I shot my load all over his chest, and damn if it wasn't a lot of cum. Chris looked at me and said that this could never happen again, but also winked when he said it, so I was a little bit confused. That was the last time I saw him.

Chapter 7

DANNY

I went a few weeks without being on my apps because I had made the decision to really start working toward opening up my own practice. I couldn't be without work much longer, but also knew I'd be miserable if I went back to work for someone else. I didn't have much money saved up, but luckily my parents had told me when I left that they'd be willing to help me whenever I needed it. I thought for sure they'd hang up on me when I asked for as much as I asked for, but when I told them my plans, they were more than happy to send it.

I found a location in the Castro District. I figured this had to be the best spot to open up my practice because the gay men would surely flock to my practice for their issues. I got all the paperwork filed, spent a few weeks getting the office ready, and decided to take one last weekend to relax before getting back to seeing patients.

I decided to get back on the apps and came across this extremely handsome guy named Danny. He was about five years older, and we started chatting. He seemed like a gentleman, and I could tell he wasn't just looking for a hook-up. At this point, neither was I, because I was still fucking around with Michael. He was kind of dating someone, but we seemed to have this unspoken agreement that we would just use each other for sex until one of us got into something serious.

Danny asked if I could meet him for lunch, and I was more than happy to. He was a successful sales manager for a chain of hotels, so we spent a lot of the lunch talking about our careers. He was half Puerto Rican but looked mostly like a white guy. He was just as handsome as he was in the photos and super sweet. Our lunch went great, and I asked if he wanted to grab dinner the next night, but he said he was going out of town the following morning to visit some friends for the weekend. He said he'd love to meet back up the following week, and I was more than happy to.

Ten minutes hadn't even passed since we left lunch when he started texting me. We somehow got on the topic of cuddling, and I said that I bet he was an amazing cuddler. I kind of saw this as my invitation and asked if he wanted me to come over early in the morning before his flight for some cuddle time. "I swear I'm not looking for a hook-up, just some good cuddles," I messaged him. He said he'd like that and texted me his address.

The next morning, I showed up at his house around 4am. He said he needed to get up and start getting ready for his flight at around 6am, so that would give us a solid two hours of cuddling. He texted me the code for his door so I could just go in and slip right into bed. He had a really cute house that he was renovating, but I made my way through and found his bedroom in the back. When I walked in, he appeared to still be sleeping, but he had kicked the covers off of him, and I noticed that he was sleeping naked. I kept my clothes on and slipped into the bed and kind of backed up into him so we could spoon. I must have woke him because he wrapped his arm around me and pulled me close.

I could feel his dick rub against my ass, but I couldn't tell if he was hard or not. I laid there for a few minutes but knew that I wasn't going to fall asleep. I had lied about just wanting to cuddle. I wanted to fuck. I started moving my ass and rubbing it against his dick to see if he would notice. Within seconds, he started kissing on the back and side of my neck. I put my hand on his leg behind me and started rubbing it and started rubbing my ass a little faster.

I took my shirt off and was about to turn over so I could start kissing him, but he pushed me forward onto my stomach and kind of held me down. I could feel him get up from the position he was lying in, and then he started pulling my shorts and briefs off. Before I knew it, he had his tongue so deep in my hole that it immediately made my cock hard. When we were at lunch, he had mentioned that he was an ass man, but I didn't think he'd be doing this so soon. He licked my hole for a while, and I could feel how wet it was. He then rolled over onto his back and told me to sit on his face. I got on top of him and saw his big cock standing straight up, so while he was eating my ass, I went down and started sucking on his dick.

I'm not sure how I always lucked out getting men with perfect dicks, but somehow, I did. Danny really was an ass man because whenever I tried to get up, he would pull my ass back down to his face. I kept sucking on his dick, and after a few minutes, I told him I wanted him to fuck me. I got up and could tell that we weren't going to need any lube because my ass was soaking wet from him eating it. He stayed on his back, and I sat on that dick as fast as I could.

Danny's cock felt so good inside of me, and I could tell he wanted to take control. He grabbed onto my hips and started thrusting his cock in and out pretty fast. I rode him for a few minutes before he flipped us over so that I was on his back and he was on top. He grabbed both of my ankles and held them in the air spread apart, and that's when I could feel how truly big his cock was. That position was always a bit intense for me. He pushed his cock deep inside of me, and I held onto his chest while he was fucking me. He was a bit of a dirty talker too, asking if I loved his dick and saying, "This ass is mine." I never really had anyone talk dirty to me, but I definitely liked it.

I was stroking my cock while he was fucking me, and he didn't even give me any warning that he was about to cum. He pulled his dick out and got a bit on top of me and stroked his cock until he started shooting his load all over my face and chest. I kept jerking my cock and rubbed his cum on my chest and into my mouth with my other hand. He leaned down and started licking his cum off my chest while I was still stroking my dick, and I felt him reach down and stick his fingers in my ass. That definitely helped because I instantly started shooting my load when he did that. He turned his face toward my dick and opened his mouth to try and catch my cum in his mouth.

I knew I was going to like cuddle time with Danny and knew that we were going to end up dating, which we did for a few months. Jackie decided to host a family dinner, and I invited Danny over, along with some of our friends. During dinner, Danny started talking about how he thought humans evolved from aliens, and we all lived in outer space. After that conversation, I never spoke to him again.

Chapter 8

CHARLIE –
MY FIRST TOP

I wasn't really sure how to market my practice, or what I should do to build up my client base, so I made a bunch of flyers and started distributing them to all the local businesses in the District. I figured if a gay man was going to get a referral for therapy, why not find it on one of those random bulletin boards at a gay bar or doctor's office?

After a few weeks of plastering the area with advertisements, I finally had my first client make an appointment. I couldn't afford to hire any help, so I was playing every role in my office–therapist, receptionist, billing specialist, janitor–you name it. I was excited to finally be getting back into what I loved doing, and hopefully this was going to take off.

Charlie was my first patient. He was 30 years old and lived in the District. When he got to the office, I greeted him, and we went into my office to have our discussion. I asked him what brought him in to see me. He said that he had been in a relationship with another guy for the past six months, but their sex life was an issue because they are both only tops. So, whenever they wanted to have intercourse and not just blowjobs, they had to involve other guys.

I was a bit shocked. Personally, I had never met someone who only preferred one position, and I myself obviously just enjoyed sex, regardless of the position.

"What do you mean by you're only a top?" I asked him. And this is when I knew this conversation was going to get very interesting.

Author Bio

Grayson Ace has had his fair share of sexcapades, and figured why not write about them? Recently divorced, he is re-discovering himself (and plenty of hot men) and creating many new sexy adventures along the way. If you like what you see, please leave a review, and you never know....you may end up in one of the stories!

GraysonAce.com

Facebook: Grayson Ace

Instagram: graysonaceofficial

Twitter: @GraysonAce1

More Books From Grayson Ace

How I Got Here
First Year Out of the Closet
You're Only a Top?

4 Horsemen Publications
Erotica

Dalia Lance
My Home on Whore Island
Slumming It on Slut Street
Training of the Tramp
72% Match

Ali Whippe
Office Hours
Tutoring Center
Athletics
Extra Credit

Honey Cummings
Sleeping with Sasquatch
Cuddling with Chupacabra
Naked with New Jersey Devil
Beau and Professor Bestialora
The Goat's Gruff
Goldie and Her Three Beards
Pied Piper's Pipe
Princess Pea's Bed

Fantasy/Paranormal Romance

Valerie Willis
Cedric the Demonic Knight
Romasanta: Father of Werewolves
The Oracle: Keeper of the Gaea's Gate
Artemis: Eye of Gaea
King Incubus: A New Reign

J.M. Paquette
Klauden's Ring
Solyn's Body
Hannah's Heart

4HorsemenPublications.com